Can you find?

1. Where is the cat? 2. How many windows can
3. Where is the Christmas wreath? 4. How ma

1

Sticker fun

Add stickers to the scene to fill the ice rink with skaters.

Missing hats

These three busy elves have lost their hats. Draw one for each elf.

Christmas word search

Can you find all the Christmas words in the word grid?

```
k s n o w f l a k e d r e a
e a z r y c h o p i e u s t
x n b d f s w a e s c p o a
l t c a g q j t e h o b c f
r a s u c z e p i t r a o s
r e i n d e e r u d a s a k
n s u v y g j e l h t r e e
d a g w x t o s p f i u r i
c h o l l y t e h a o t o q
i e b m t c s n p i n a r f
c n c h r i s t m a s r m s
t o n g z t c s n o w m a n
w b m p i n r c i f s p e t
c s t o c k i n g u m x f g
```

snowflake Christmas tree snowman decorations
holly presents stocking reindeer Santa

How many?

Can you count how many of each of these balloons there are: red balloons, picture balloons, and balloons shaped like dogs?

Spot the difference

The children have been busy making snowmen. Can you spot six differences between them?

Colouring

Santa is delivering presents on Christmas Eve.
Colour the picture with bright colours.

_ A R _ _ _ R

_ O T _ _

_ _ N N _ _ _

D _ N _ _ _ _

_ U _ I _

_ R _ N _ _ _

Santa's reindeer

Write the name for each reindeer on the signs beneath them. Some letters are already written in to help you.

DASHER	COMET
DANCER	CUPID
PRANCER	DONNER
VIXEN	BLITZEN

_ _ I E _ _

_ _ _ _ Z _ N

6

Dot-to-dot

Join the dots to find out what goes bang.

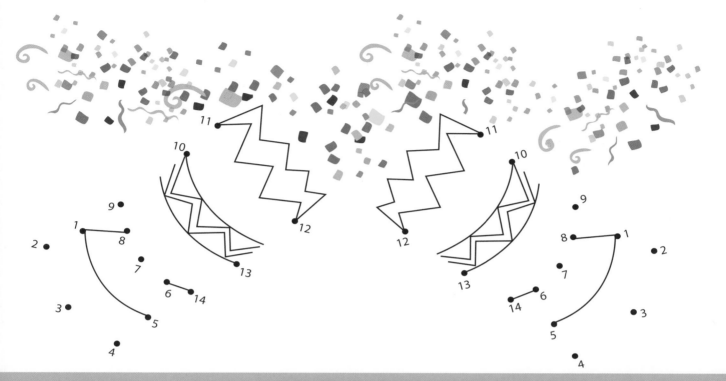

Spot the difference

Can you spot six differences between the two Christmas trees?

Spot the difference

The children are nestled in their beds on Christmas Eve.
Can you find six differences between the two pictures?

Santa Decoration

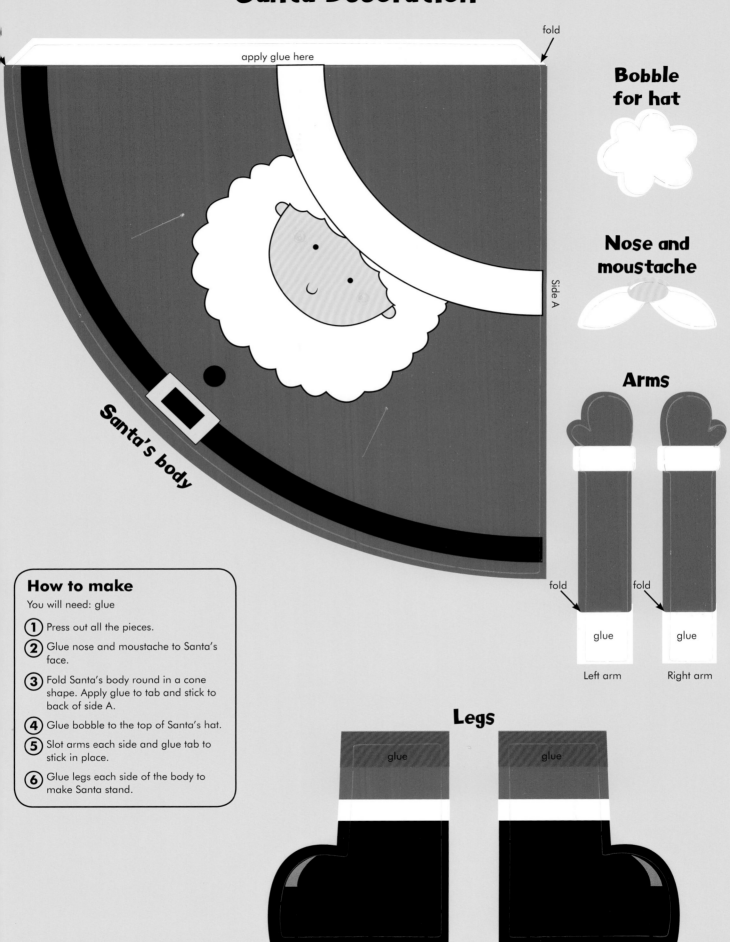

fold

apply glue here

Side A

Santa's body

Bobble for hat

Nose and moustache

Arms

fold   fold

glue   glue

Left arm   Right arm

Legs

glue   glue

How to make

You will need: glue

1. Press out all the pieces.
2. Glue nose and moustache to Santa's face.
3. Fold Santa's body round in a cone shape. Apply glue to tab and stick to back of side A.
4. Glue bobble to the top of Santa's hat.
5. Slot arms each side and glue tab to stick in place.
6. Glue legs each side of the body to make Santa stand.

Christmas present

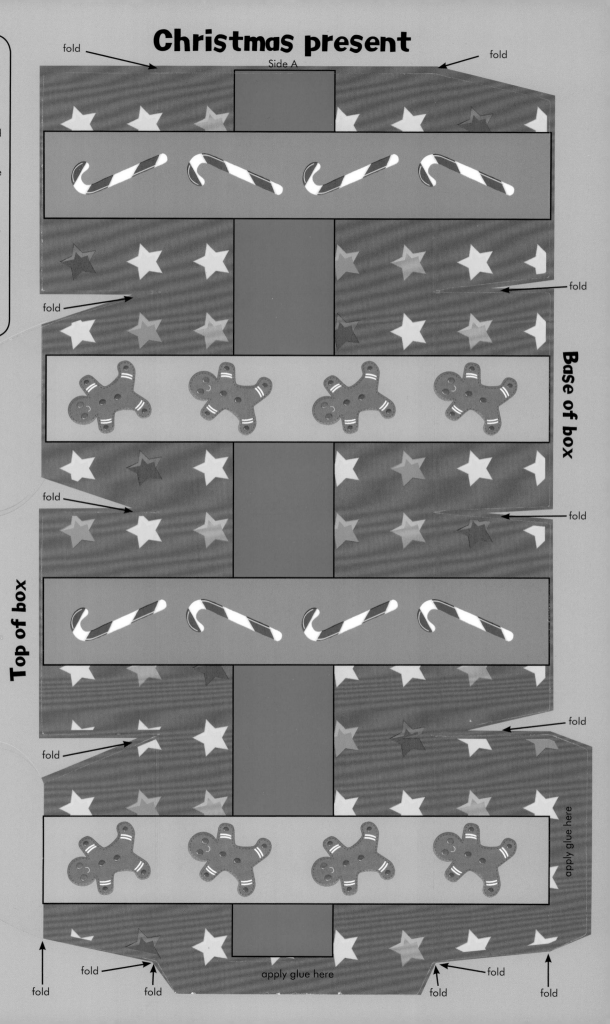

How to make

You will need: glue, and maybe some adult help

1. Press out the present carefully.

2. Fold along all the creased edges to form the box shape. Apply glue to the long tab and stick it to the back of side A.

3. When dry, fold up all the tabs at the base of the box. Apply glue to the tab and slide it into place to secure the base.

4. Fold the top tabs down and slide the two bow sections together along the slits to secure. See finished picture.

Side A

fold

fold

fold

fold

fold

fold

fold

Base of box

Top of box

fold

fold

fold

apply glue here

fold

fold

fold

fold

fold

fold

apply glue here

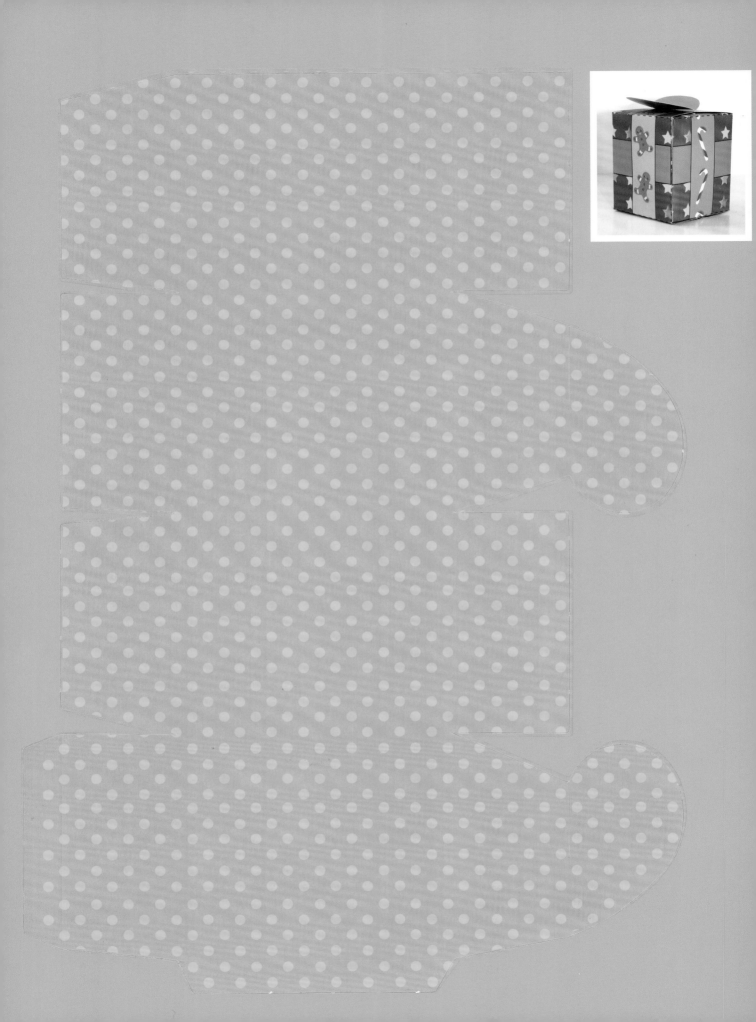

Find the stickers

Find the stickers to fill the plate with a delicious Christmas dinner.

Spot the difference

Mrs Claus is making gingerbread men.
Can you spot six differences between these two?

Colour code

The elves are busy cleaning the sleigh. Use the key to colour the scene.

TOYS

TOOLS

● GREEN	● YELLOW
● RED	● BLUE
● PINK	● GREY
● BROWN	● PURPLE

Find the stickers

Add sticker decorations to make the Christmas tree look festive.

Copy and draw

Copy the picture of the elf square by square into the grid on the right, and then colour it in.

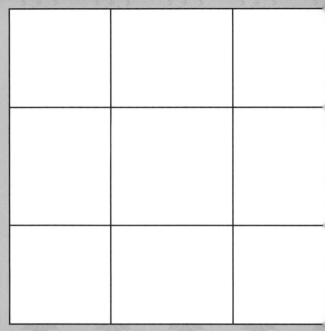

Odd one out

Which partying penguin is the odd one out?

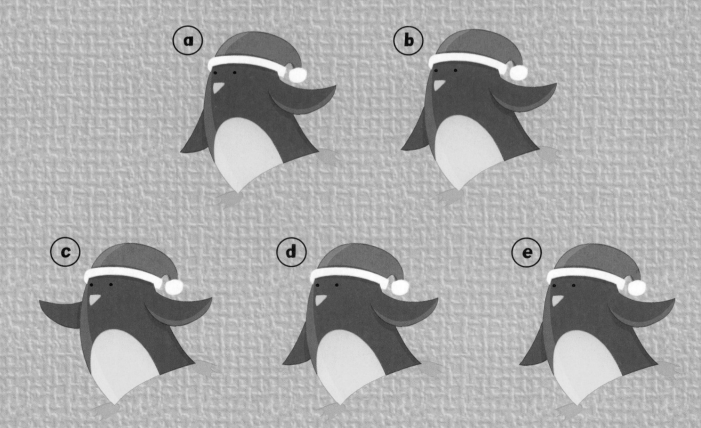

ⓐ

ⓑ

ⓒ

ⓓ

ⓔ

What comes next?

Look at the rows of objects. What comes next?
Add the correct sticker at the end of each row.

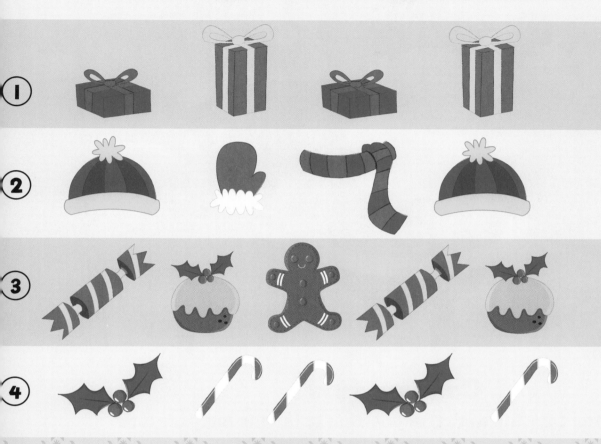

①
②
③
④

Copy and draw

Copy the picture of the robin square by square into
the grid on the right, and then colour it in.

Can you find?

Santa has lost his hat. Can you find it in this busy picture?

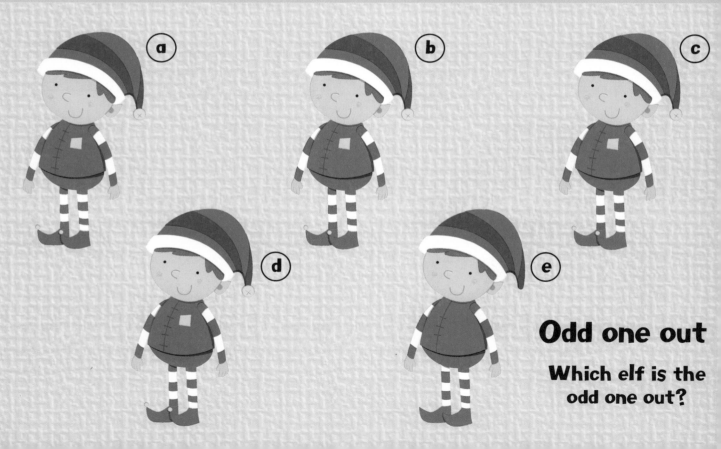

(a) (b) (c) (d) (e)

Odd one out

Which elf is the odd one out?

14

Colouring

Colour this picture in
bright colours.

Answers

Page 1
1. Under the tree
2. There are 8 windows
3. On the yellow door
4. There are 3 reindeer

Page 3

Page 4
3 red balloons, 6 picture balloons, 3 dog balloons

Page 6
Dasher, Comet, Donner, Dancer, Cupid, Prancer, Vixen, Blitzen

Page 7

Page 8

Page 9

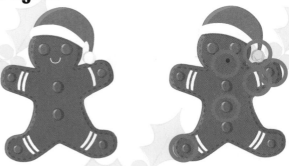

Page 12
Penguin c is the odd one out.

Page 13

Page 14

Elf e is the odd one out.